The
DOG

SQUAD

THE SHOW

Books by Clara Vulliamy

THE DOG SQUAD: THE NEWSHOUND

THE DOG SQUAD: THE RACE

THE DOG SQUAD: THE SHOW

*The Marshmallow Pie series
in reading order*

MARSHMALLOW PIE THE CAT SUPERSTAR

MARSHMALLOW PIE THE CAT SUPERSTAR: ON TV

MARSHMALLOW PIE THE CAT SUPERSTAR: IN HOLLYWOOD

MARSHMALLOW PIE THE CAT SUPERSTAR: ON STAGE

*The Dotty Detective series
in reading order*

DOTTY DETECTIVE

THE PAW PRINT PUZZLE

THE MIDNIGHT MYSTERY

THE LOST PUPPY

THE BIRTHDAY SURPRISE

THE HOLIDAY MYSTERY

For Celia and Bert, always best in show,
with love xx

First published in the United Kingdom by
HarperCollins *Children's Books* in 2024
HarperCollins *Children's Books* is a division of HarperCollins*Publishers* Ltd
1 London Bridge Street
London SE1 9GF

www.harpercollins.co.uk

HarperCollins*Publishers*
Macken House, 39/40 Mayor Street Upper
Dublin 1, D01 C9W8, Ireland

3

ISBN 978–0–00–856547–3

Clara Vulliamy asserts the moral right to be identified as the author and
illustrator of the work.
A CIP catalogue record for this title is available from the British Library.

Typeset in Aldus LT Std
Printed and bound in the UK using 100% renewable electricity at
CPI Group (UK) Ltd

This book contains FSC™ certified paper and other controlled
sources to ensure responsible forest management.

For more information visit: www.harpercollins.co.uk/green

The

DOG

SQUAD

THE SHOW

CLARA VULLIAMY

HARPERCOLLINS
CHILDREN'S BOOKS

THE NE

Top local stories! What'

THE DOG SQUAD -
ACE REPORTERS

SHOUND

! ☆ News and reviews!

Outfits for dogs~
special feature!
Page 4

QUIZ! How well do you
know different dog breeds?
Page 6

Chapter One

BOOM!

I hear thunder outside, followed by a bright flash of lightning. There's more thunder, closer and louder this time. And then the rain starts, big splashy drops on the window.

Wafer, my dog, is frightened by loud noises. He buries even deeper under his blanket, with only his trembly nose poking out. He makes a small, sad whining noise.

'Don't worry,

Wafer,' I say, scooping up both him and his blanket into a big hug. 'It's just a storm – it will be over soon.'

But at that moment – OH NO!– all the lights go out.

My big brother, Wes, who has been watching music videos on TV, GROANS as the screen goes blank.

'It's a power cut!' calls Mum from the kitchen.
'Hang on – I'm on my way!'

She comes into the room, carrying a big lamp. My little sister, Macy, is hanging on to Mum's skirt, her eyes wide.

We look out of the window. Every house on our street, every flat in the block opposite and all the streets beyond are completely dark. Even the streetlights are off.

'I can't make my pasta bake now, I'm afraid!' says Mum. 'How about a candlelit picnic tea instead?'

Mum lights three big candles, and finds some party napkins in the kitchen drawer. It all looks really pretty.

We have tortilla chips and dips, tiny tomatoes and leftover sausage rolls. Everything feels different and exciting.

At bedtime, I fetch a couple of extra blankets from the chest in the hallway for Wafer's bed, which is next to mine. He settles down peacefully. I share a bedroom with Wafer AND Macy. It's only a small room, and quite a squash. Usually, we have a night light, but it's not working at the moment because of the power cut.

'I'M not scared of the dark,' announces Macy, getting out of her bed and climbing into mine, 'but Vera, Chuck and Dave are!'

I sigh. These are her three imaginary friends.

Although they aren't real, whenever Macy talks about them, somehow the room feels even more crowded.

I have an idea. I fetch my own torch that I keep in an old shoebox, and me and Macy wriggle under the duvet. We pretend we are in a tent, camping.

'The rabbits are fast asleep in their burrows,' I whisper, 'and the cows are fast asleep in their barn . . .'

'Where do the lions sleep?' asks Macy loudly. 'And the bears, and the kangaroos?'

I ponder this, because I have absolutely NO IDEA. Luckily, I see her eyes beginning to close, and I persuade her to go back into her own bed.

I lie in the dark, listening to the rain and the wild wind bashing against the window. I snuggle down cosily under the covers, until my eyes begin to close too.

Chapter Two

The next morning, it's still raining, although the worst of the storm has passed. I try my bedside light, but it doesn't work. The electricity is still not back.

'School is closed for the day,' Mum tells us at breakfast. 'Macy, Wafer, Eva – you'll have to come to the diner with me.'

The Sunny Side Up Community Diner where Mum works has its own back-up generator, making it the perfect place for people to come to during a power cut. Mum is rushed off her feet, serving a constant supply of steaming-hot drinks and delicious warm toasties.

Wafer looks up from a crust he has found on the floor, wagging his tail cheerfully. He is the first to see that our best friends, Simone and Ash, have turned up too.

'Hey!' I call out.

'Hey, Eva!' they both call back.

There's something else you need to know about us. We are not just best friends. We are BRILLIANT reporters! We have our very own newspaper, called **THE NEWSHOUND** – investigating stories, uncovering secrets, solving mysteries. If something important is happening, one thing's for sure . . . the Dog Squad – that's us! – are on the case.

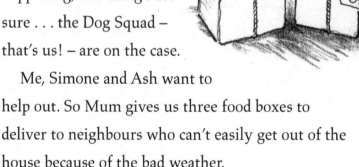

Me, Simone and Ash want to help out. So Mum gives us three food boxes to deliver to neighbours who can't easily get out of the house because of the bad weather.

'Come on, Wafer. You can come with us,' I say. 'We'll have a run around the park afterwards!'

Wafer knows a handful of words now. On hearing the word 'park', he jumps up eagerly.

I help him into his smart new raincoat, which has a pattern of dogs, cats, ducks and umbrellas. It changes colour when it gets wet.

We walk along, carrying one box each, circling around the giant puddles on the pavement. Wafer, in particular, is NOT a fan of getting his paws wet.

The first box is for Hannah across the road, who

has a new baby. The second is for Mrs Kravets, who has been in hospital recently with a broken ankle. And the third is for old Mr Brent. Mum always puts a little something in the box for his dog, Lucky, too; today it's a packet of beef Crunchers. We leave each box on the doorstep and give a friendly wave through the window.

Heading back down the high street towards the park, we pass Happy Tails Rescue – the animal shelter who looked after Wafer before he came to live with us. Sally, the owner, is hurrying in and out with buckets.

'Oh, hi!' she says. 'And hello, Wafer!'

'Hello!' we reply.

'What's going on?' I ask, looking at the buckets sloshing with water.

'We've had storm damage, I'm afraid,' she tells us. 'A big hole in the roof.'

'Oh NO!' says Simone. 'What about all the animals?'

'I'm not sure what will happen,' Sally says, shaking her head. 'We're all very worried. We can't afford to fix the roof – it will cost five hundred pounds, and we just don't have that much. Unless we can raise the money, we will have to close.'

We look at each other and gasp.

We reach the park and let Wafer have a run around while we talk. Branches have been blown down during the night and scattered across the grass, which is great news for Wafer. He chooses a stick five times wider than he is to carry around.

'Happy Tails HAS to stay open,' says Ash, frowning. They have a very determined look on their face.

23

Yes, that's right – they! Ash is non-binary, not a boy and not a girl, just an amazing, fantastic human! So, instead of 'she' and 'her' or 'he' and 'him', when we are talking about Ash we all say 'they' and 'them'. They always wear the cute badge Simone made for them to remind everybody.

'I wish we could help Happy Tails,' says Simone, 'but I don't know how . . .'

I'm not sure how we can help either. WE certainly don't have that much money. I think really hard . . . and then – oh! The perfect idea pops into my head!

'Could we put on a fundraising event?' I suggest.

'Sounds good!' says Ash. 'What kind of event?'

It starts raining again so we decide to head back. We are still trying to come up with the ideal fundraiser.

'A talent show?' suggests Simone.

'Ooh, yes!' I agree. 'That would be great!'

I glance down at Wafer, trotting alongside us. He has insisted on bringing the very long stick with him. He gets stuck trying to fit through a narrow gap in the alleyway, but eventually finds a way.

'You're a very clever dog, Wafer!' Ash tells him.

'Yes, he is!' I say proudly. 'Hang on . . . How about a DOG talent show?'

'Ha – brilliant!' laughs Simone.

'I LOVE it!' agrees Ash. 'We could raise loads of money. And not only that – it has all the ingredients for a GREAT story in *THE NEWSHOUND!*'

HOLE IN THE ROOF AT HAPPY TAILS!

What will happen to the animals if the shelter is forced to close?

Chapter Three

The first thing I hear when I wake up the next morning is the kettle whistling in the kitchen, which means Mum is making herself a cup of coffee. The power has returned! So I reckon I'll be going back to school today.

Sure enough, soon I'm hurrying over to join Ash and Simone in the playground as we line up with the rest of our class. There are twigs and branches everywhere, brought down in the storm. Mr Fuller, our teacher, is helping to clear up, gathering huge handfuls of leaves and dumping them in a pile in the corner.

I look around. There's so much space in our playground, and that gives me another idea.

'Let's ask Mr Fuller if we can put on the fundraiser here, at school!' I say.

At form-time, when we all get to share our news, we tell Mr Fuller about the disastrous hole in the roof at Happy Tails, and that we'd like to raise the money to help.

'So we want to put on a talent show!' says Ash.

'A DOG talent show!' adds Simone.

Mr Fuller chuckles. 'Well, I think it's crazy, but I like it. When?'

'As soon as possible!' I reply.

'Okay. I'll book the playground for next Saturday morning, which is a week tomorrow,' Mr Fuller tells us. 'One important thing, though. This opportunity should be open to the whole class – anyone who wants to can join in.'

The entire room erupts into a hubbub of

excitement. Great! Everyone seems keen.

Almost everyone, that is . . . Max sits back in his chair, arms crossed, sneering as usual. 'Bet it all goes wrong,' he mutters.

We ignore him. Everybody else is talking at once, discussing ideas enthusiastically in small groups at their different tables. There's so much chat, I can't even hear what is being said.

Me, Ash and Simone share a table, so we turn to each other and start making plans. We get out our reporters' notebooks to jot things down. As Ash said yesterday, this could make a really good story for **THE NEWSHOUND** too.

'We have a target of five hundred pounds to raise,' Ash reminds us.

I have a lightbulb moment. 'I know!' I say. 'How about making one of those fundraising charts that looks like a thermometer?'

'We can add paw prints going up the thermometer as the money comes in!' Simone adds, doodling a little drawing in her sketchbook to explain. She's the artistic one.

Ash and me lean over to admire the doodle. 'Cool!' we both agree.

The bells goes. We need to leave it for now. I stand up.

'Come to the library on Monday lunchtime for our next planning meeting!' I announce to the class in my loudest voice.

That's odd. As we file past to go to our first lesson, I notice that Mr Fuller is on his hands and knees under his desk, as if he's searching for something on the floor. But he smiles up at us.

'That went well!' he says. 'Off to a good start!'

After school, we call in at Happy Tails. We find Sally on the doorstep, bundling some sodden-wet newspaper into a binbag. We tell her all about the fundraising dog talent show. She is DELIGHTED.

'Oh, wow, thank you!' she exclaims. 'Thank you SO MUCH.'

At the corner of the high street, we all go our separate ways. I walk on home, feeling very pleased with how it's all going. *And*, I think to myself, *we have plenty of time.*

Chapter Four

At the weekend, I make a start on the thermometer money chart. I ask Mum if she's got any BIG bits of paper. She finds a roll of wallpaper on top of a cupboard.

'You can use the back of this!' she says, cutting off a long piece, nearly as tall as me. It's just right. I lay out my paint pots, brushes and a jam jar of water on the floor.

Wafer scampers over to see what I'm doing, sniffing around, very eager to get involved. He's always really nosy – literally, in fact. He pokes his nose into a paint-pot and knocks it over,

sending dollops of red all over my
chart.

I dive for some kitchen towel to wipe
it up, and give Wafer's face a good clean
too. Mum cuts me another piece of the
wallpaper, so I can begin again.

'I know you're trying to help,' I tell Wafer,
giving him a nice scratch behind his ear. 'But, to be
honest, you are getting in the way a little bit . . .'

On Monday morning at form-time, Mr
Fuller is a bit down in the dumps. He has
let his tea go cold, and he's hardly touched
his digestive biscuit.

'I lost my wedding ring,' he tells us. 'I'm not sure
when, or where . . .'

Oh, so that's what he was searching for on
Friday. We're all really sad for him! Mr Fuller is
married to our friend, the vet from Pet Planet. We
all promise to look out for the ring.

At lunchtime, we wolf down our food
as quickly as possible. Simone always
brings a packed lunch, but me and Ash
have school dinners. We
plead with Simone to share
even just a crumb of the sticky
treacle loaf her dad has made,
because it is INCREDIBLE.

Then we hurry over to the library for our first
proper planning meeting for the fundraiser. Meera,

our school librarian, greets us from her desk with a cheery wave. EVERYONE from our class turns up! Fantastic! There aren't nearly enough chairs, so some of us sit on the floor.

I unroll the thermometer money chart, and proudly hold it up for everybody to see. At that very moment, right opposite me, Harry holds up another thermometer money chart, almost exactly the same. He and his friends Eddie and Damsa, who all

sit at the same table,
must have had the
same idea as us.

Oh.

It all goes a bit
quiet. Harry rolls up
his chart and puts it
back in his bag.

'Okay, never
mind!' I say as
cheerfully as I can.
'The next thing we
need is POSTERS!
We want to advertise
the event, encourage
people to come – and
bring their dogs
to enter the talent
show!'

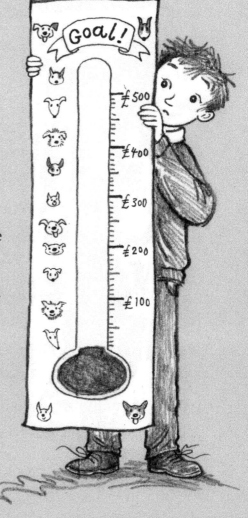

When we get back to the classroom, Mr Fuller looks up from marking a big pile of books. 'Everything going okay?' he asks.

'Yes,' we tell him. 'Everything's great!'

I get rained on, walking home from school. The weather is still unsettled, and the sky is grey. I hope it clears up by Saturday.

After tea, I take out my notebook and my tub of best pens. I sharpen my special double-ended pencil – one end blue, the other end red. **DOG TALENT SHOW!** I write at the top of the page. Then I sit for a while, wondering what to put next.

Wafer is playing close by with his precious long stick. No one can persuade him to part with it – he takes it everywhere. Giving it an over-enthusiastic waggle, he knocks over my pens, sending them flying through the air.

'Oh, Wafer,' I sigh, gathering them up again,

crawling under chairs to find the last few. After that, I can't seem to concentrate on anything.

Chapter Five

At the second meeting in the library, not as many people turn up.

'Oh well,' I say, 'at least we all get a chair to sit on!'

I see Amy at the back, holding a pen and a blank piece of paper. She seems keen, but not exactly sure what to do.

'So, where have we got to?' I carry on. 'Oh yes – posters!'

Silence. Everyone is looking at me. With a sudden sinking sensation in my stomach, I realise what has happened.

This is the second time we haven't worked together as a team. Yesterday, we ended up with two groups accidentally making a thermometer chart, when we only needed one. This time, we have the opposite problem. We talked about making posters, but everyone thought another group would do it – so NO ONE has.

The rest of the meeting doesn't go well, either. Some people, like Amy, are waiting to hear what jobs they can get on with. But it's impossible to arrange anything over the noise of others all shouting out at the same time.

'Let's have a huge light show with holograms and lasers!'

'No, let's have fireworks!'

'Let's get a famous pop star to come!'

Ash lets out an exasperated sigh. I put my head in my hands.

Simone looks frustrated too. 'These aren't the right kind of ideas at all,' she says.

I notice that Amy still doesn't have anything written down. I wonder if maybe she seems a bit sad. But the bell goes, so we have to finish and head back to our classroom.

I have an uneasy feeling that everything is starting to go wrong.

Mr Fuller is busy emptying out his desk drawers, and searching through piles of odds and ends. His wedding ring is still missing. He looks over at me with a kind expression. 'It's okay to ask for help, you know!'

'No, it's all fine,' I tell him. We don't need any help. We will fix this ourselves. We are the Dog Squad – we can do anything!

For the rest of the day, though, we don't make any progress at all. After school, we walk home together, as we always do. This would usually be a really good time to chat about our plans. But today we are all very quiet.

At tea, Mum says, 'I hope everything is going well with the talent show!'

I push my baked beans around the plate with my fork, and don't answer.

She glances across the table at me. 'Anything I can do?' she offers.

I shake my head.

I know I should be busy. This week is hurtling
by REALLY FAST. We should be further ahead with
our preparations by now.

The weird thing is, the more I worry, the less I'm
able to get on with anything.

Chapter Six

It's Wednesday already.

At lunchtime, Simone offers to share her home-made ginger snaps with me and Ash, but none of us feels very hungry. We are impatient to get to our next planning meeting.

We each find a seat in the library, and wait. And wait. But this time no one turns up.

It's all falling apart. We have gone beyond worry now. I feel SICK with panic.

'We haven't done anything,' I say. 'We still haven't put any posters up! We don't have any dogs to enter the show!'

'Should we cancel?' Simone asks.

'But we can't let Happy Tails down!' exclaims Ash.

'No, we can't,' I agree. 'They were SO pleased and grateful when we told them about it.'

We got this wrong, I think to myself. *We can't do it all by ourselves, after all.*

I get to my feet, decisively.

'It's time to talk to Mr Fuller,' I say.

We tell Mr Fuller everything, and he calls an emergency meeting for everybody.

'You have three days left. It's very tight, but you can do it!' he says. 'Make a list of what needs doing, and divide up tasks according to people's particular skills.' He gives us a meaningful look. 'There are a lot of talented people in this room,' he adds, 'if you just look around.'

He's right, I think. We are so used to doing things on our own, we didn't appreciate that the others were trying to help, and DO have skills to offer. We haven't been good at teamwork. I feel bad. I can see that Simone and Ash do too. We are determined to do this properly.

We make a list. Then
we all sit in a circle, and go
round to each person one
by one.

'You are really brilliant at maths,' Ash says to Sumaya. 'You and me will run the business side of things. You can be in charge of the money!'

Sumaya gives Ash a double thumbs-up.

'You're great at art, Harry!' says Simone. 'We could make the posters – let's start right now!'

'Sounds good!' Harry replies.

'Amy,' I say, 'we are going to have a LOT of dogs in the playground. We need to take really good care of them. Shall we do this together?'

Amy nods eagerly, all smiles.

'Can I be stage manager?' pipes up Vijay. 'I've been in quite a few shows before. I know a lot about it!'

'Yes!' I reply. 'Fantastic!'

And soon all the jobs are given out. Scarlett and Yuri are decorating the stage. Lexi will be the presenter, because she has an incredibly loud voice. Rose, Amir and Damsa will be the welcome committee, because we need really friendly people at the gate on the day. Everyone else who's keen to help out finds a group to join.

Sumaya and Ash	MONEY	
Harry and Simone	POSTERS	DOG TALENT SHOW!
Amy and Eva	DOGS' QUIET CORNER	
Vijay	STAGE MANAGER	
Scarlett and Yuri	STAGE DECORATIONS	
Lexi	PRESENTER	
Rose, Amir and Damsa	WELCOME COMMITTEE	

'Without you we don't have a show!' I say to the whole class.

'We are depending on you!' adds Simone.

Everyone grins back at us, feeling happy and encouraged.

Max is hanging back, as usual, not in the circle.

On impulse, Ash says, 'Max, how about you?'

'What?' he answers, looking surprised.

'Would you like to join in?'

'I'm not sure . . .' he begins uncertainly. 'Maybe.'

'What would you like to do?' Ash asks.

'I don't know . . . I'll think about it.'

I don't have much confidence. All I know for certain is that Max spends a lot of time on his own. But Ash is good at seeing things in people that others miss.

Chapter Seven

With only two days to go, everything starts to go RIGHT.

We all meet in the playground early on Thursday morning, before school. Mr Fuller is already here, talking to the caretaker, who will be responsible for building the stage. Meera arrives too, with the posters she has printed for us in the library. They look amazing – Simone and Harry have done a great job.

Mr Fuller sent an email to everyone's families yesterday, and it's all arranged. We will go out in small groups along the High Street, each with a pile of posters to hand out. Mr Fuller and Meera will stand on the corner, making sure that everything goes well.

Posters go up in all the local shops and cafés. Everyone is delighted to help.

Me, Ash and Simone call in at Wags and Whiskers, the day-care centre for dogs while their owners are at work. Sam, who looks after the dogs, is in reception, welcoming the first customers who have started to arrive. Wafer is already here, playing a game of tug with his friends. Mum dropped him off early, before going to the diner. I'm so glad he's having a lovely day. He is very excited to see me!

Sam takes a poster, and his face breaks into a huge smile.

'A dog talent show – what a fantastic idea!' he says. 'We have some very talented dogs here. LOADS of people will want to come!'

Sam puts the poster in the window. Wafer is keen to help, jumping up and getting a muddy pawprint on the poster, and a piece of sticky tape stuck to his nose.

WAGS and WHISKERS

Dog Talent
Show!

THIS SATURDAY!!

A young woman arrives on her bicycle, with a small fluffy white puppy in the basket.

'What fun!' she says. 'We'll be there!'

Another customer is wrestling a massive wolfhound in through the door.

'Us too!' he adds.

'You'll be serving refreshments, I expect,' Sam says to us.

REFRESHMENTS! We hadn't even thought of that! I hastily scribble down a reminder in my notebook.

'Have you thought about selling snacks for the dogs?' Sam goes on. 'We could help with that, if you like?'

'YES, PLEASE!' we all reply together.

Next stop is Pet Planet.

'Ah yes, I've been hearing all about the show,' the vet says. 'I was hoping you'd be calling by with one of these!' He enthusiastically takes a poster for the window, and a couple of extras for the noticeboard.

On the way out, we bump into Wafer's friend, Herman, who is an elderly sausage dog.

'We'll come!' says his owner. 'When he's in the mood, Herman can be persuaded to SING – if you can call it that,' she adds, rolling her eyes. 'Bring your ear plugs.'

It looks great, seeing posters up in almost every window as we walk back along the high street towards school.

At form-time, everyone is buzzing with more ways to raise even more money.

'Shall we have a cake stall?' Tom suggests.

'Genius!' I say. 'Who can make cakes?' A forest of hands goes up.

Some of the sporty kids in class have another brilliant idea.

'How about an obstacle course for dogs?' says Jamila. 'Different styles of jumps, tunnels, ramps, a see-saw . . . we could charge fifty pence a go!'

'Awesome!' says Simone.

'We could call it the dogstacle course,' Ash chips in, giggling.

Jamila and her friends hurry away to find Miss Cooper, our PE teacher, and ask her to lend us some equipment.

At teatime, I have a proper catch-up with Mum. She has made us corn on the cob, which is one of my favourites, except when it gets stuck between my teeth. Wafer is home now too, tucking into *his* tea.

'You seem much more cheerful today,' says Mum. 'I'm so glad!'

'Yes, it's going well!' I tell her, wiping a bit of melted butter off my chin. I get out my notebook,

and turn to the page on refreshments. 'Lots of
people are making cakes for a cake stall . . .' Macy
looks up from her corn, always alert to the magic
word CAKE . . . 'and Wags and Whiskers are
bringing snacks for the dogs. But maybe we need

drinks for everyone too?'

'Good work!' says Mum admiringly. 'The diner could provide a pop-up café, serving teas, coffees, cold drinks . . . What do you think?'

'That would be amazing!' I say. We spend the rest of the time talking about our favourite cold drinks, and decide that home-made lemonade would be perfect.

Mum writes it all down in her notebook, with the Sunny Side Up logo on the front. It feels really nice, seeing our notebooks together on the kitchen table.

The days are whooshing past, though . . . *Can we get it all done in time?*

Chapter Eight

It's Friday afternoon. The dog talent show is TOMORROW!

'Lessons are cancelled, folks!' announces Mr Fuller. 'It's all hands on deck!'

Mr Fuller doesn't call us 'boys and girls' because, as Ash is non-binary, it wouldn't even be true.

He calls us 'folks', or sometimes, for a joke, 'you horrible beasts'.

The classroom is bustling with activity. Last-minute decorations are being made, with lengths

of paper bunting stretched out across the room. Programmes are written and rushed to the library to be photocopied. An old empty biscuit tin is found in a cupboard, and converted into a money-collecting box.

It's one big happy team effort, and so much more fun with everyone joining in.

'We need more dogs, though!' I say. Miss Cooper pops her head round the door with an armful of plastic hoops and

cones for the dogstacle course.

'I'm coming with Primrose,' she tells us. 'She's really tiny, a teacup chihuahua, but she's very good at yoga!'

'My mum has a corgi called Hettie,' says Mr Fuller. 'I think she can balance a biscuit on her nose. I'll bring her along.' He looks out of the window. 'Fingers crossed for good weather,' he adds. The sky is still full of grey clouds. It's been raining on and off all day.

When I get home from school and walk into the kitchen, a delicious smell hits me. Macy, having overheard yesterday that everyone is making cakes, has insisted on joining in. With Mum's help, she has baked a big batch of cupcakes and is about to start decorating them.

Macy is a chatterbox. She loves to give a running commentary on everything she's doing. 'First, a handful of sprinkles,' she says, 'then a little bit more squirty cream . . .' Very soon the whole place is a gooey, creamy, sugary multicoloured chaos.

I'm not the only one who has noticed the inviting smell. Wafer peeps round the door, pushes it open and comes in.

'Hello, you!' I say, giving him a hug.

Again, Wafer is almost too keen to help. He jumps up on to a chair to investigate, his waggy tail knocking the pot of sprinkles off the table. Now he is 'helping' by licking them up off the floor. His sprinkle-covered nose looks like a cupcake itself.

'It's not his fault,' I say to Mum, sighing, as I brush the sprinkles up into the dustpan. 'He really wants to help. He does try to be a good boy.' Wafer knows more and more words these days. But he

hasn't understood the full meaning of what I was
saying. Because at the mention of 'GOOD BOY!' he
looks up, pleased and proud.

That night, in bed, I go through my notebook,
checking every detail one last time. *Well,* I think to
myself, *we've done everything we possibly could.*
We're as ready as we can be.

But, just as I'm drifting off to sleep, I jolt awake
with a sudden, awful thought:

What about Wafer?

I've been so busy that I haven't prepared anything
for him to do in the
show! I'd completely
forgotten!

I sit up in bed.
I rack my brains
for anything he
can do . . . Does he
have any particular

talents? He wanted to help with making the thermometer but got paint everywhere. He loves his big stick, but that isn't really a special skill. He thought he could help with the cake-decorating, but instead he knocked over the sprinkles. To be honest, he has been mainly getting in the way. But he is so keen to be involved with everything the Dog Squad does, and he tries so hard to be good.

It's all SO last-minute, though. Too late. I can't think of anything.

Chapter Nine

The day of the show has arrived!

The first thing I do is rush to the window and look outside. YAY! At last, the rain has stopped and the sun has come out.

I grab some breakfast to have on the go, and set off for school, bringing Wafer with me. Cleverly I manage to distract him with a piece of banana, so he forgets to bring his special stick. I have a feeling that today could be chaotic enough as it is.

Everyone is here, bright and early, keen to help set up. Simone and Harry are supervising the decorations.

'The playground is already looking really
FANTASTIC!' I say.

Scarlett and Yuri smile down from the chairs
they are standing on to pin up bunting across the
stage, holding one end each. Eddie, Amir and

Damsa are positioned by the gate, ready to hand out
programmes. Ash and Sumaya are setting
up a small table with two chairs, so they can take
the money and give out change from the money-
collecting box.

Jamila and her friends are busy arranging the dogstacle course. Miss Cooper's tiny dog, Primrose, is trying it out. She looks very dainty as she trots along the ramp, and can jump surprisingly high.

'She isn't nearly heavy enough for the see-saw, though!' Miss Cooper laughs.

I am just coming out of the caretaker's shed with an armful of blankets when I see it. Oh WOW! I don't mind admitting that my mouth falls open with surprise. It's the most AMAZING dog photo booth!

And it's being set up by . . . MAX!

It's basically three sides of a big cardboard box, with a painted background inside – mountains and trees and fluffy white clouds in a bright blue sky. Max has borrowed his dad's Polaroid camera, and put up a little sign that says: 'PUP PORTRAITS £1 each!' There's a choice of dressing-up clothes and accessories for the dogs to wear.

'Max, this is incredible,' I tell him.

He grins shyly.

'Can we be your first customers?' I ask.

Mr Fuller, rushing past with a stepladder, stops to admire the Polaroid photo of Wafer, who looks VERY snazzy in a sparkly crown and pink feather boa. Mr Fuller did say there were lots

of talented people in our class, but, as he glances at Max, clearly impressed, I can tell that even he was not expecting this.

'I'd like to be a photographer when I'm older,' Max tells us.

'You already are!' I say.

By now, crowds of people are starting to arrive, and not just dog owners. Lots of kids from other classes have turned up to support us too, as well as parents and neighbours. They all pay their entry fee, and visit the side attractions – the photo booth, the dogstacle course, the cake stall – and the money

GOAL! ☆
☆   ☆
£500   ☆
         ☆
£400   ☆
         ☆
£300   ☆

£200
         ☆
£100
☆   ☆
☆   ☆
☆

thermometer starts to climb. Simone is busy adding the pawprints.

It's getting very busy now, and noisy. That makes it even more important for the dogs to have a calm, peaceful space to relax in, tucked away from the hurly-burly. Me and Amy are organising the Quiet Corner.

'I'll make sure there is plenty of fresh water for the dogs to drink,' Amy says.

'That's great,' I reply. 'And we have lots of comfortable cushions and blankets.'

Wafer has found a cosy spot to curl up in. His friend Herman is already here too, lying on his back, fast asleep and snoring.

'That's his favourite pose, the Belly-up,' says his owner. 'Knowing him, he'll probably sleep through the whole thing. At least we might be spared his singing.'

Sally from Happy Tails comes over to say hello. She looks around. 'Oh, my – this is all so wonderful!' she exclaims.

'Yes, it really is!' I say, looking around too. I just hope we can raise all the money they need.

And now it's time. Vijay is waving his stage-manager's clipboard above his head, calling out last-minute instructions. Lexi, our presenter, gathers everyone to the stage. There is a hush of excitement.

Lexi announces, in her loudest voice, 'LET THE SHOW BEGIN!'

Chapter Ten

There are no winners and losers in our show. Instead, it's a chance for the dogs to enjoy themselves, performing their talents just for fun.

The first act is a dog who can skateboard. She puts her front paws on to the board and uses her back paws to run along until she has enough speed to jump on completely. She circles the stage, looking very cool in her glow-in-the-dark, go-faster striped jacket.

Next is a dog who can perform all sorts of different tricks – paw-shake, ballerina, roll over – in exchange for tiny treats the owner gives him from her pocket. SO clever!

Now here is Hettie, Mr Fuller's mum's corgi,
who – it's true! – CAN balance a biscuit on her nose!

An enormous Great Dane is next to bound on to
the stage.

'He doesn't really have a talent as such,' his owner tells us, laughing, 'but I'm sure you'll agree he has a lovely smile.' And he does!

After a very successful first half, we have an

interval. There's a big rush on the snacks and drinks.

The diner pop-up café is super busy, serving coffees, teas and iced lemonade. Mum, pouring from the world's most enormous teapot, looks over at me and smiles proudly.

The cake stall is set up alongside the pop-up café. Home-made cakes – of the most weird and wonderful shapes and sizes – are going down a storm. Lots of my classmates are helping out. But the best salesperson, putting a lot of pressure on customers to buy loads of cakes and over-pay generously, is Macy. I don't know why I'm surprised. She has a very strong character, and it's impossible to say no to her once she's set her mind on something.

There's no point in even trying.

I take Wafer over to the Wags and Whiskers stall. We study the Doggo Delights Menu for ages – there is so much to choose from! Fruity freezies, unsalted 'pupcorn', dog-safe ice creams . . . In the end I treat Wafer to a dairy-free 'puppuccino' – a small paper cup with whipped coconut cream and a strawberry on top.

'BONE APPÉTIT!' Sam jokes.

The vet from Pet Planet arrives. 'Sorry I couldn't get here any sooner,' he says. 'We've had so many patients in today!' He gives his husband's hand a little comforting squeeze. Mr Fuller is still sad about his missing wedding ring.

The vet is very friendly. He walks around, stopping to chat with everyone.

'I haven't got a dog to bring, I'm afraid,' he tells us. 'We have cats at home instead!'

'So do I!' says Ash. The vet and Ash discuss cats

for a while. Ash tells him all about their cat, Frank.

'Well,' the vet says, looking around, 'this is all an absolute triumph!'

He has a compliment for everybody.

'The money is

very well organised,' he says. Sumaya and Ash are delighted.

'This, erm, unusual-shaped cake is DELICIOUS.' Macy beams. 'The decorations are fabulous.' Simone and Harry give each other a high five.

'And I am especially impressed with how well the dogs are taken care of, which is the most important thing of all. Well done, Eva and Amy!'

Ash and Sumaya are working really hard at their little table, collecting the money and giving change.

I watch the thermometer money chart anxiously.

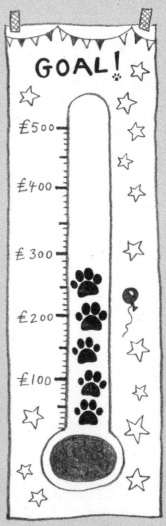

Pawprints are constantly added, the level steadily climbs and climbs . . .

But it hasn't reached the target. It's still not enough.

Chapter Eleven

The second half of the show is just as good as the first.

Miss Cooper's tiny dog, Primrose, presents her very graceful yoga poses. The wolfhound from Wags and Whiskers dances with his owner . . . and a pair of dogs play a toy piano, AND take a bow.

There's just one sad thought hanging over the day, though. I have a pang of regret that Wafer isn't performing. I feel I've really let him down.

Wafer has been happily watching the show for a while, but now he's getting a bit restless. He trots over to the big pile of leaves and branches in the corner, tidied away last week after the storm.

I wonder if he's hoping to find another stick, as he wasn't able to bring his with him today.

At that moment, something seems to catch his eye. He starts madly digging, leaves and twigs flying everywhere. If there's one thing I know, it's to trust Wafer's instincts. I hurry over. Simone and Ash, immediately alert, come running across too. It's a **DOG SQUAD** thing: we are reporters – it is our job to notice *everything*.

And then we see it too. Something shiny, glinting in the debris. Wafer brings it to us, holding it gently in his mouth . . . and oh! There it is!

MR FULLER'S WEDDING RING!

Mr Fuller is overjoyed. 'I thought it was gone forever!' he says, giving the ring a quick wipe and putting it back on his finger. 'It must have fallen off when I was helping to clear up all those leaves on Monday morning!'

Of course, this is Wafer's special talent – his amazing powers of sight and doggy curiosity! How could I have forgotten? Mr Fuller's ring would have been lost forever if Wafer hadn't spotted it. He ALWAYS wants to help, and this time he really, really has.

Mr Fuller's husband, the vet, is delighted too. He gets up on to the stage.

'I have an announcement!' he says. 'To show our gratitude to Wafer and his human friends for finding our missing wedding ring, Pet Planet will match any sum of money raised today.'

We can hardly believe it! Ash, Simone and me give each other a big hug, and we all hug Wafer too. The money is doubled, just like that!

Ash and Sumaya quickly dash back to their table to work out the maths. Simone updates the thermometer chart with more and more pawprints. There's so much to add that in the end we need both charts, my one and the one Harry made, taped together. Thank goodness we have two!

We all crowd around, everyone in suspense . . . the pawprints go up, up, up . . .

But is it enough?

I pick up the money chart, and look at it. Simone and Ash peer intently over my shoulder. Without saying a word, we grab Sally from

Happy Tails and get up on to the stage.

We hold the thermometer chart up high for everyone to see. THE TARGET HAS BEEN REACHED!

The crowd bursts into applause. Sally looks as if she might cry with happiness. 'We have enough money to fix the Happy Tails roof,' she says. 'A HUGE thank you to everyone – the Dog Squad have saved the day!'

There is more applause. All the kids in our class are cheering and whooping. When Wafer hears the words DOG SQUAD, he jumps up on to the stage too, barking loudly, tail wagging ecstatically. Everyone laughs and cheers even more.

I look at Wafer, tearing around joyfully. It's so sweet

that these are the words he knows and loves best of all. *This is what makes him extra special*, I think to myself. *He is SO PROUD to be in the Dog Squad.*

Wafer's cheery barking wakes up Herman, who gets slowly to his feet and begins 'singing'. He raises his head to the sky and starts to howl. That sets the other dogs off. Now they are ALL barking, yapping, howling, whining – some running about, others storming on to the stage. There's just no stopping them.

It is ABSOLUTE CHAOS. A choir of dogs, all singing together. I bet you can hear it miles away! What a finale!

Chapter Twelve

The show is over. Everything is cleared up and packed away. With everyone helping, it takes hardly any time at all.

After we have all said our goodbyes, people start to drift home.

'Do you want to come over for a while?' I ask Simone and Ash.

'Yes, please!' says Ash.

'We need to make a start on our story for **THE NEWSHOUND** too!' Simone reminds us.

As we walk along, Wafer stops and begins to rummage in some bushes.

'Ah yes, this is the Magic Doughnut Bush,' I

explain to the others. 'Wafer once
found half a doughnut here,
so he has to investigate
EVERY TIME we go past,
even though he hasn't
found anything since.'
Wafer carries on
searching for AGES.

'Sorry, pal,' I say when he
is finally persuaded to move on. 'You win some, you
lose some, I'm afraid!'

At home, we finish off the lemonade that Mum
has brought back. Macy is piling a plate high with
leftover cakes, leaving only the very squashed,
misshapen ones for us. 'These are for Vera, Chuck
and Dave!' she says, hurrying along the hallway
in the direction of our bedroom. I know it's no use
trying to stop her.

We budge up on the sofa, while Wafer takes

up most of the space, sprawled out on his blanket
having a nap. I get out my reporter's notebook and
flip through the pages.

'This is a big story – there's a LOT to fit in,' I say. 'The storm, the hole in the roof at Happy Tails, the dog talent show . . .'

'We have TWO stories, in fact!' says Ash. 'There's the mystery of Mr Fuller's wedding ring too!'

'Wafer really saved the day,' says Simone. Even in his sleep, Wafer stirs slightly when he hears his name.

'He really did,' I agree. 'He helped Mr Fuller – and so Pet Planet helped us!'

Mum puts her head round the door. 'Look!' she says. 'I've found a lovely frame for that Polaroid photo of Wafer.'

'Oh, thanks, Mum!' I say. 'It's great! I'm going to keep it on my bedside table with all my most precious things, so I can look at it EVERY DAY.'

On Monday, at lunch, Simone has brought ginger snaps again, which is good news, because this time we are really hungry.

'Let's get straight to work on **THE NEWSHOUND**,' suggests Ash when we've finished eating.

'Good idea,' agrees Simone.

'We need to get this edition out super quickly,' I say as we stack our trays on the trolley. 'Everyone keeps asking me when they can read it!'

We hurry over to the library, get out our notebooks and write our story.

☆ ✏ 📷 ☆ ✏ 📷 ☆ ✏ 📷

PRESS

THE NE

Top local stories! What

A HAPPY ENDING
FOR HAPPY TAILS

HAPPY
TAILS

OPEN!

HAPPY

£500

SHOUND
! News and reviews!
Wafer saves the day!
Page 2
Mr Fuller's wedding ring~
LOST AND FOUND!
Page 4

A HAPPY ENDING FOR HAPPY TAILS!

During last week's awful storm, DISASTER struck at Happy Tails Rescue, causing a big hole in the roof! The Dog Squad immediately wanted to help, and decided to put on a fundraising show. But no ordinary show . . . A DOG talent show!

We soon realised, though, that we couldn't do it by ourselves. Luckily, we have the most AWESOME classmates, who all pitched in to make the whole day a HUGE success. Together, we raised enough money to fix the Happy Tails roof.

The dogs in the show entertained us with their amazing talents. ALL of our classmates wowed us with their many different skills. Everybody is special. Everyone is good at something.

And, finally, a big shout-out for Wafer, and his flair for mystery-solving. Poor Mr Fuller, our teacher, was so sad, because he lost his wedding ring. He thought it was gone forever. But clever Wafer found it, buried in a pile of leaves!

'Wonderful!' says Meera, and she prints it out for us. Mr Fuller calls by, eager to see a finished copy. He takes one from the pile for him, and another for his mum.

'Do you know what impressed me most?' he says.

'Was it Hettie balancing a biscuit on her nose?' I ask.

'Well, OBVIOUSLY!' he laughs. 'But even more than that . . . you three made sure that everybody had their moment to shine. Well done.'

'What a day!' says Ash, as we sort *THE NEWSHOUND* into bundles, ready to distribute to our impatient readers.

'What a show!' says Simone.

'The Dog Squad and friends,' I say. 'What a team!'

And, we all agree, we are already excited for our next adventure!

106

Check out more of Clara's books...

The Dog Squad

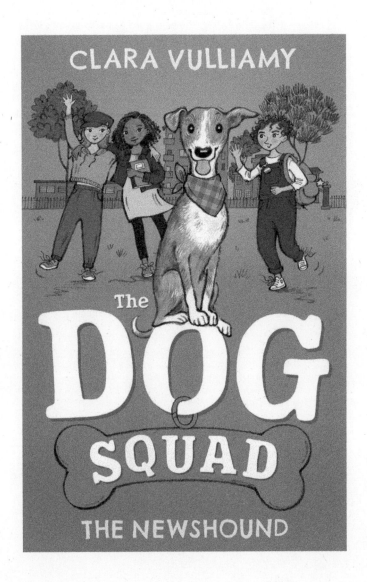

CLARA VULLIAMY

The
DOG
SQUAD
THE NEWSHOUND

CLARA VULLIAMY

The
DOG
SQUAD

THE RACE

Dotty Detective

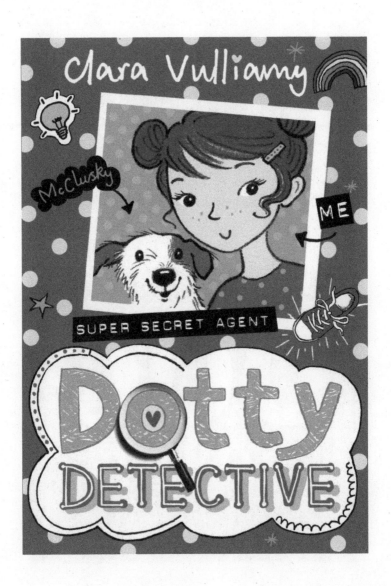

Clara Vulliamy
ME
McClusky
THE PAW PRINT PUZZLE
Dotty
DETECTIVE

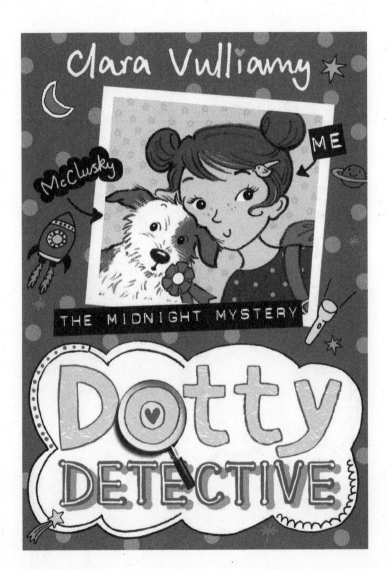

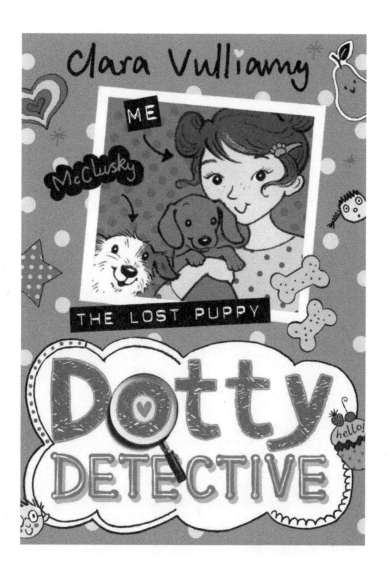

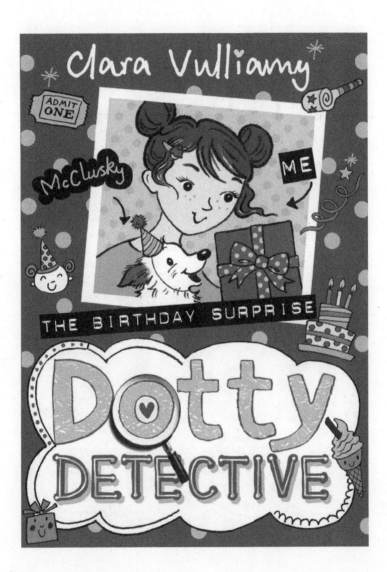

Marshmallow Pie
the Cat Superstar

Marshmallow Pie the Cat Superstar on TV

Clara Vulliamy

Marshmallow Pie the Cat Superstar in Hollywood

Clara Vulliamy

Marshmallow Pie the Cat Superstar On Stage

Clara Vulliamy